For Janet and Neil

Macmillan Publishing Company
866 Third Avenue, New York, NY 10022

Originally published in
Great Britain by
Hutchinson Children's Books,
London, England.

Printed and bound in Italy
First American Edition 1990

Library of Congress
Cataloging-in-Publication
Data is available.

ISBN 0-02-717775-0

10   9   8   7   6   5   4   3   2   1

THE WINTER HEDGEHOG

ANN AND REG CARTWRIGHT

Macmillan Publishing Company
New York

ONE cold, misty autumn afternoon, the hedgehogs gathered in a wood. They were searching the undergrowth for leaves for their nests, preparing for the long sleep of winter.

All that is, except one.

The smallest hedgehog had overheard two foxes talking about winter. "What is winter?" he had asked his mother.

"Winter comes when we are asleep," she had replied. "It can be beautiful, but it can also be dangerous, cruel, and very, very cold. It's not for creatures like us. Now go to sleep."

But the smallest hedgehog couldn't sleep. As evening fell he slipped away to look for winter. When hedgehogs are determined, they can move very swiftly, and soon the little hedgehog was far from home. An owl swooped down from high in a tree.

"Hurry home," he called. "It's time for your long sleep." But on and on went the smallest hedgehog, until the sky turned dark and the trees were nothing but shadows.

The next morning, the hedgehog awoke to find the countryside covered in fog. "Who goes there?" called a voice, and a large rabbit emerged from the mist. He was amazed to see a hedgehog around with winter coming.

"I'm looking for winter," replied the hedgehog. "Can you tell me where it is?"

"Hurry home," said the rabbit. "Winter is on its way, and it's no time for hedgehogs."

But the smallest hedgehog wouldn't listen. He was determined to find winter.

Days passed. The little hedgehog found plenty of slugs and insects to eat, but he couldn't find winter anywhere.

Then one day the air turned icy cold. Birds flew home to their roosts and the animals hid in their burrows and warrens. The smallest hedgehog felt very lonely and afraid and wished he was asleep with the other hedgehogs. But it was too late to turn back now!

That night, winter came. A frosty wind
swept through the grass and blew the last
straggling leaves from the trees. In the
morning the whole countryside was covered
in a carpet of snow.

"Winter!" cried the smallest hedgehog.
"I've found it at last." And all the birds flew
down from the trees to join him.

The trees were completely bare, and the snow sparkled on the grass. The little hedgehog went to the river to drink, but it was frozen. He shivered, shook his prickles, and stepped onto the ice. His feet began to slide and the faster he scurried, the faster he sped across it. "Winter is wonderful," he cried. At first he did not see the fox, like a dark shadow, slinking toward him.

"Hello! Come and join me," he called as the fox reached the riverbank. But the fox only heard the rumble of his empty belly. With one leap he pounced onto the ice. When the little hedgehog saw his sly yellow eyes he understood what the fox was up to. But every time he tried to run away he slipped on the ice. He curled into a ball and spiked his prickles.

"Ouch!" cried the fox. The sharp prickles stabbed his paws and he reeled toward the center of the river, where he disappeared beneath the thin ice.

"That was close," the smallest hedgehog cried to himself. "Winter is beautiful, but it is also cruel, dangerous, and very, very cold."

Winter was everywhere: in the air, in the trees, on the ground, and in the hedgerows. Colder and colder it grew until the snow froze under the hedgehog's feet. Then the snow came again and a cruel north wind picked it up and whipped it into a blizzard. The night fell as black as ink and he lost his way. "Winter is dangerous and cruel, and very, very cold," moaned the little hedgehog.

Luck saved him. A hare scurrying home gave him shelter in his burrow. By morning the snow was still falling, but gently now, covering everything it touched in a soft white blanket.

The smallest hedgehog was enchanted as he watched the pattern his paws made. Reaching the top of a hill, he rolled into a ball and spun over and over, turning himself into a great white snowball as he went. Down and down he rolled until he reached the feet of two children building a snowman.

"Hey, look at this," said the little girl. "A perfect head for our snowman."

"I'm a hedgehog," he cried. But no one heard his tiny hedgehog voice.

The girl placed the hedgehog snowball on the snowman's body and the boy used a carrot for a nose and pebbles for the eyes. "Let me out," shouted the hedgehog. But the children just stood back and admired their work before going home for lunch.

When the children had gone, the cold and hungry hedgehog nibbled at the carrot nose. As he munched, the sun came out and the snow began to melt. He blinked in the bright sunlight, tumbled down the snowman's body, and was free.

Time went on. The hedgehog saw the world
in its winter cloak. He saw bright red berries
disappear from the hedgerows as the birds
collected them for their winter pantries. And
he watched children speed down the hill on
their sleds.

The winter passed. One day the air grew
warmer and the river began to flow again.
A stoat, who had changed his coat to winter
white, changed it back to brown. Then the
little hedgehog found crocuses and
snowdrops beneath the trees and he knew it
was time to go home. Slowly he made his way
back to the wood.

From out of every log, sleepy hedgehogs were emerging from their long sleep.

"Where have you been?" they called to the smallest hedgehog.

"I found winter," he replied.

"And what was it like?" asked his mother.

"It was wonderful and beautiful, but it was also . . ."

"Dangerous, cruel, and very, very cold," finished his mother.

But she was answered by a yawn, a sigh, and
a snore—and the smallest hedgehog was fast asleep.